Barbie & The Diamond Castle

By Mary Man-Kong
Based on the original screenplay by Cliff Ruby & Elana Lesser
Illustrated by Rainmaker Entertainment

Special thanks to Rob Hudnut, Shelley Dvi-Vardhana, Vicki Jaeger, Monica Okazaki, Christine Chang, Jennifer Twiner McCarron, Shawn McCorkindale, Pat Link, and Walter P. Martishius

❦ A GOLDEN BOOK • NEW YORK

Published in the United States by Golden Books, an imprint of Random House Children's Books, a division of Random House, Inc., 1745 Broadway, New York, NY 10019, and in Canada by Random House of Canada Limited, Toronto. No part of this book may be reproduced or copied in any form without permission from the copyright owner. Golden Books, A Golden Book, A Little Golden Book, the G colophon, and the distinctive gold spine are registered trademarks of Random House, Inc.
www.goldenbooks.com   www.randomhouse.com/kids
Educators and librarians, for a variety of teaching tools, visit us at www.randomhouse.com/teachers
Library of Congress Control Number: 2007939383   ISBN: 978-0-375-87508-3
Printed in the United States of America   10 9 8 7

Long ago, there were two best friends who lived together in a humble cottage in the woods. Liana and Alexa didn't have much money or fancy dresses, but they shared everything—especially their love of singing!

One day, the friends found two perfect heart-shaped
stones and made them into beautiful necklaces—one for
each of them.

"Best friends today, tomorrow, and always!" Liana and
Alexa both closed their eyes and made a wish.

They didn't notice that the necklaces began to glow. . . .

Later that day, Liana and Alexa met an old woman near their cottage. The woman was very hungry, so they offered her all the food they had. For their kindness, the woman gave them a small mirror.

Back home, the girls began to sing their favorite song—and were astonished when they heard a third voice join them. It was coming from the mirror!

The two friends discovered that a girl named Melody was hiding inside the mirror. Melody came from a magical place called the Diamond Castle, where the guardians of music, called muses, lived. The Diamond Castle was the birthplace of all music, and every time someone sang a new song, a precious jewel would appear on the sparkling palace.

Melody told the girls about a very selfish muse named Lydia who wanted to rule the entire kingdom. Playing her enchanted flute, Lydia had tried to take over the Diamond Castle. Luckily, the other muses had magically hidden the castle and given Melody the only key to find it.

Lydia had been very angry. She played her flute and turned the muses to stone. Melody escaped and hid in the old woman's mirror. And she didn't utter a sound until she heard the two girls singing.

That was all Lydia's helper, Slyder, needed to find her. He heard Melody singing with the girls and alerted Lydia.

Alexa and Liana wanted to help Melody return to the
Diamond Castle and rescue the muses. Melody told them
that they had to travel west, toward the Seven Stones.
The girls quickly set off.

Along the way, Alexa and Liana found two lost
puppies, whom they named Lily and Sparkles.

Unfortunately, the girls also ran into a mean troll who wouldn't let them continue their journey unless they could solve his riddle: "What instrument can you hear but not see or touch?"

"Your voice—when you sing," Liana answered correctly.

Furious, the troll disappeared in a puff of smoke! Alexa and Liana quickly went on their way.

Not long after, a dark shadow filled the sky. It was
Lydia, riding on Slyder's back!

"Give me the mirror and you can have all this," the
evil muse said, offering glittering jewels to Alexa and Liana.

But they wouldn't betray their friend Melody.

Angered, Lydia tried to turn the girls into stone with her enchanted flute. Fortunately, Alexa and Liana were protected by their stone necklaces.

The girls and the puppies ran and ran until they reached
a beautiful manor on a hilltop. Inside were tables full of
food and closets filled with pretty dresses. The manor was
everything the girls could ever wish for.

"We can't stay," Liana said. "Melody's in trouble."

But Alexa didn't want to go. She was hungry, tired, and a little afraid.

Sadly, Liana left the manor with Melody and Sparkles.

Alexa couldn't believe that Liana had chosen Melody over her! She tore off her necklace and threw it on the floor.

Just then, Lydia appeared. She had created the manor as a trap!

"Your spell won't work," Alexa declared.

"Brave words for a girl who no longer wears her necklace," Lydia said, and played an eerie tune on her flute.

Alexa soon fell under Lydia's spell—and revealed that
Liana and Melody were heading for the Seven Stones.
"After them!" Lydia ordered Slyder.

Slyder quickly found Liana and the mirror and brought them back to Lydia's lair. The evil muse demanded that Melody reveal the location of the Diamond Castle. When Melody refused, Lydia ordered the spellbound Alexa to walk toward a pit of molten lava!

Melody had to save Alexa. "You win, Lydia," she said sadly. "I'll take you to the Diamond Castle."

As Lydia left with Melody, Slyder pushed Liana and Alexa into the bubbling lava pit! Luckily, the girls landed safely on a narrow ledge.

Liana heard barking from above. It was Lily—with Alexa's stone necklace.

"Best friends today, tomorrow, and always!" Liana put the necklace on Alexa, and Alexa slowly opened her eyes and smiled. The spell was broken!

Liana and Alexa soon found Lydia in a misty glade. When the evil muse spotted the girls, she cast a spell on a pond and it became a churning whirlpool. "Now come to me!" Lydia commanded as she played her enchanted flute.

Pretending to be mesmerized, Liana and Alexa walked toward the whirlpool. Then, at the last moment, Liana grabbed the flute from Lydia and threw it into the swirling water.

"No!" Lydia cried. She leapt after her flute and was pulled down into the whirlpool's murky depths.

With Lydia gone, Liana and Alexa used Melody's key
to find the Diamond Castle—the key was a special song!
The girls began to sing, and the Diamond Castle
magically appeared. As they passed through the castle's
jeweled halls, their dresses turned into beautiful gowns and
Melody was set free from the mirror.

Just then, Lydia rode into the castle on Slyder! Melody quickly grabbed the Diamond Castle's enchanted insruments and handed them to Liana and Alexa. The girls started to play and sing in perfect harmony.

"No!" Lydia cried.

The girls' beautiful music turned the evil muse and Slyder into stone!

The beautiful music broke Lydia's evil spell. The muses were saved! For their bravery and kindness, Liana and Alexa were appointed Princesses of Music and invited to live at the Diamond Castle. But instead, they decided to return with the puppies to their humble cottage.

"Best friends today, tomorrow, and always!"